Be Thankful for
TREES

Harriet Ziefert ● Brian Fitzgerald

Red Comet Press ● Brooklyn

For Banba
—B.F.

HARRIET ZIEFERT has written over two hundred books for children. She is also the publisher of Blue Apple Books. She lives and works in the Berkshires, Massachusetts.

BRIAN FITZGERALD is an internationally recognized, award-winning illustrator who lives and works in Ireland.

Be Thankful for Trees
Text copyright © 2022 Harriet Ziefert
Illustrations copyright © 2022 Brian Fitzgerald

Published in 2022 by Red Comet Press

Library of Congress Control Number: 2021945279
ISBN (HB): 978-1-63655-020-6
ISBN (EBOOK): 978-1-63655-024-4
22 23 24 25 TLF 10 9 8 7 6 5 4 3 2

First Edition
Printed in China

RedCometPress.com

FIRST

A tree is food.

Would life be satisfying
without trees?
It would not!

Sweet sap to gather...

Pecans to pick...

Nuts, berries, bark,

to crunch, munch, and lick.

Leaves for a koala...

Bamboo shoots for a bear...

A giraffe stretches up
for an acacia tree's fare.

Apples and syrup for you...

Cherries and chocolate for me...

People and animals
are fed tree by tree.

SECOND

A tree is comfort.

Would life be good
without trees?
It would not!

What gives you a seat...

a floor for your feet...

a place you can sit
with your family to eat?

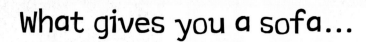
What gives you a sofa...

some comfy chairs...

a way to the attic—
with pull-down stairs?

A baby's cradle...

A double-decker bed...

A dining table with
a mom at the head.

Places to sit,
places to slumber.
A tree is lumber!

THIRD

A tree is music.

Would life be melodious
without trees?
It would not!

Pianos and bongos...

A violin and bow...

The moan of a cello,
lonesome and low.

The pum-pum of a drum...

A guitar's twangy strum...

Tree wood makes music
zing, ping, and hum.

FOURTH

A tree is art.

Would life be beautiful
without trees?
It would not!

Paper for drawing…

Recipes for cooks...

Signs, magazines,
and glorious books!

With brushes and paint...

Or drawn by yourself...

A creation on paper—
displayed on a shelf!

We surely all can agree—
a tree inspires creativity!

FIFTH

A tree is recreation.

Would life be fun
without trees?
It would not!

Paper kites swirling...

Boats floating by...

Tall trees reaching up
help us see sky.

Oars and paddles...

Benches with slats...

Skateboards, balance beams,
and long wooden bats.

Wooden toys
are lots of fun,
creative play
for everyone.

SIXTH

A tree is home.

Would life be comfy
without trees?
It would not!

Sturdy branches to swing from...

hang on, or rest…

A perfect forked branch
holds a neat little nest.

Habitat for a frog...

A burrow in roots...

"This big hole is mine,"
say an owl's loud hoots.

Protection and shelter...

under a wide leafy dome...

A place to sleep—
a tree is a home!

SEVENTH

A tree is life.

Would life be possible
without trees?
It would not!

Storms, fires, floods...

All kinds of construction...

Trees need protection
from man-made destruction.

No place for a bird,
no shade and no green…

Trees make the earth rich
and keep our air clean!

Explore a cool forest
with its pine-scented breeze.

Just remember, forever,

BE THANKFUL FOR TREES!